FUN AT THE ZOO
MAZE
BOOK

Zady Barnett

ACTIVITY BOOKS

Book Design By Zady Barnett
Illustrations by Various Artists

Published by 621 Creative Limited
www.621creative.com

First Edition Printed August 2022
Second Edition February 2023

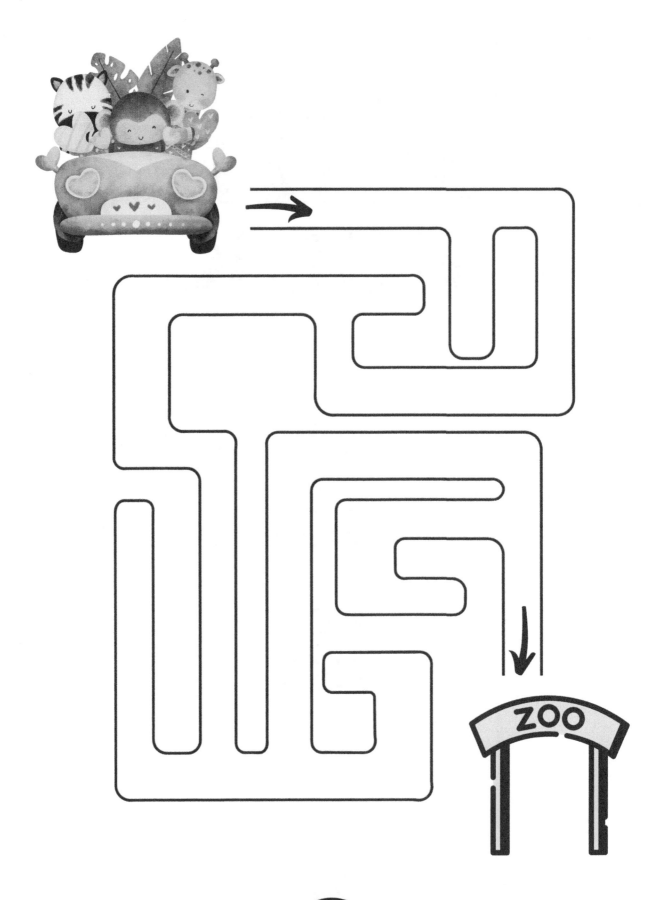

1

3

4

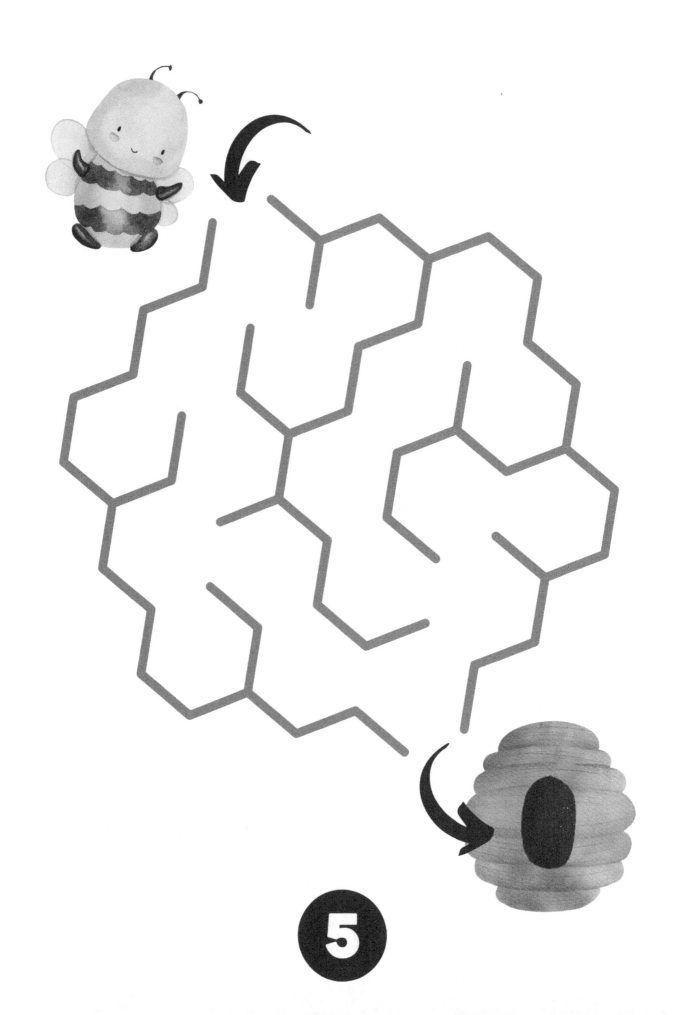

5

7

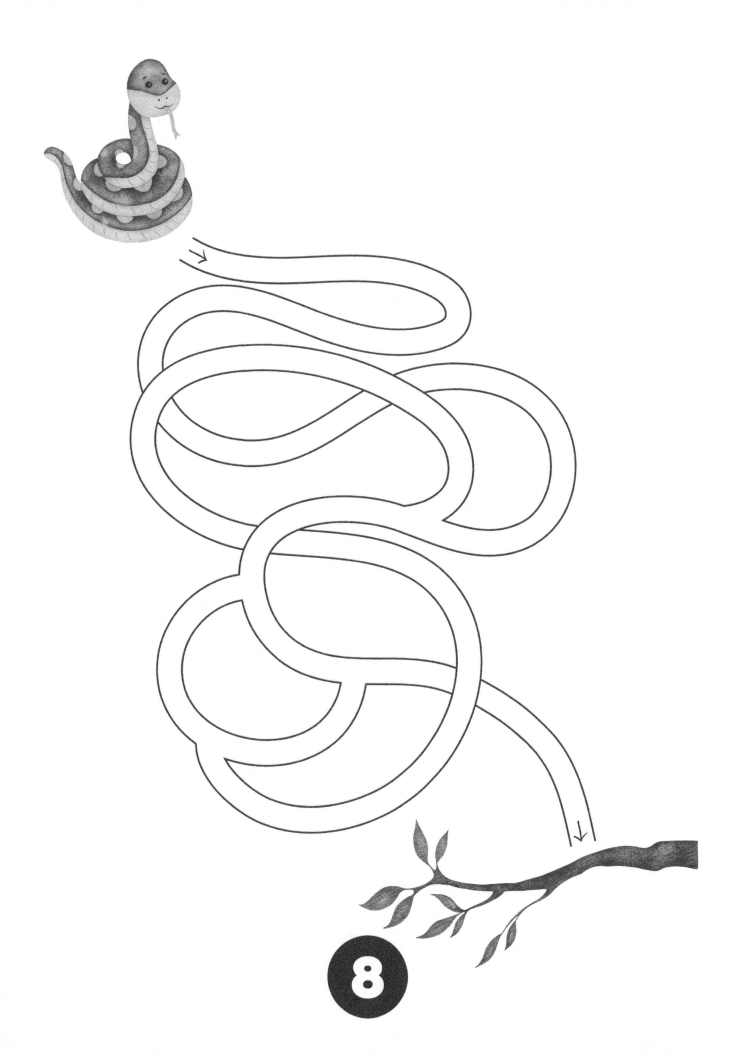

9

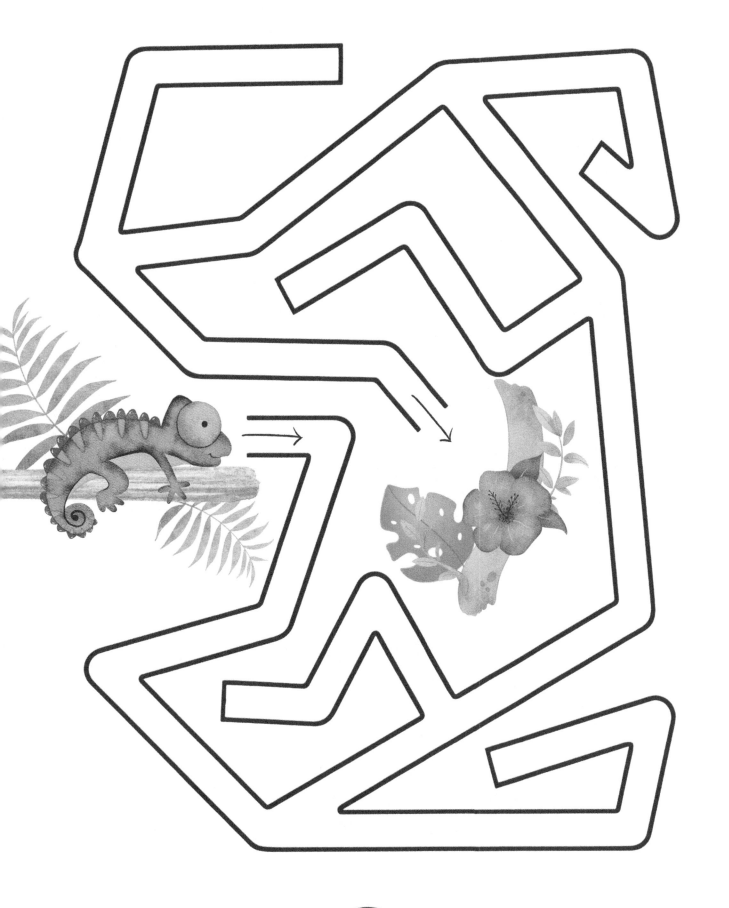

10

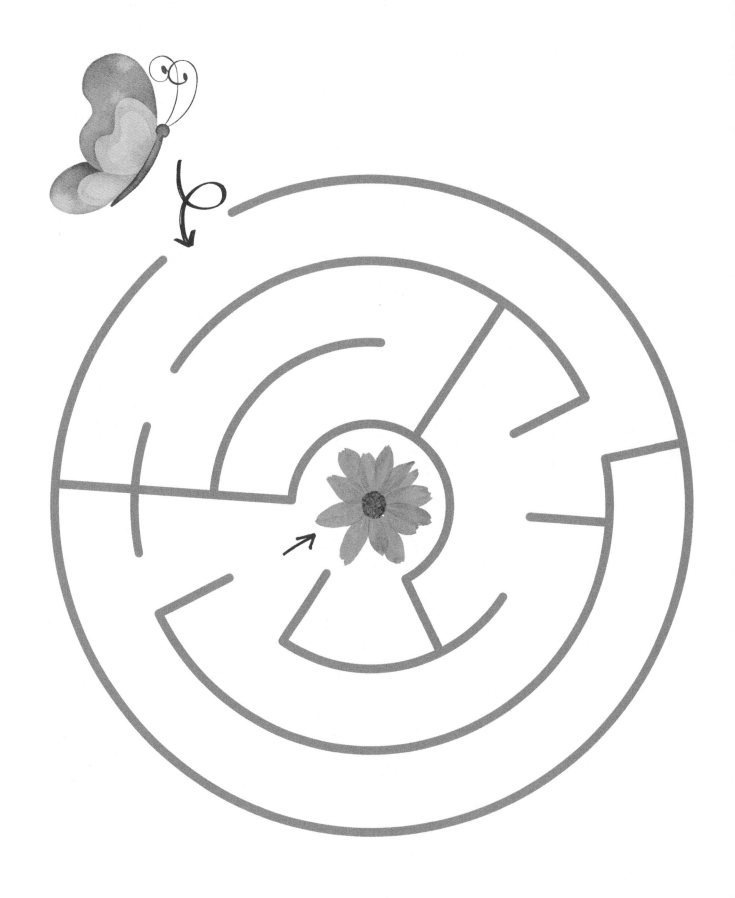

11

12

13

14

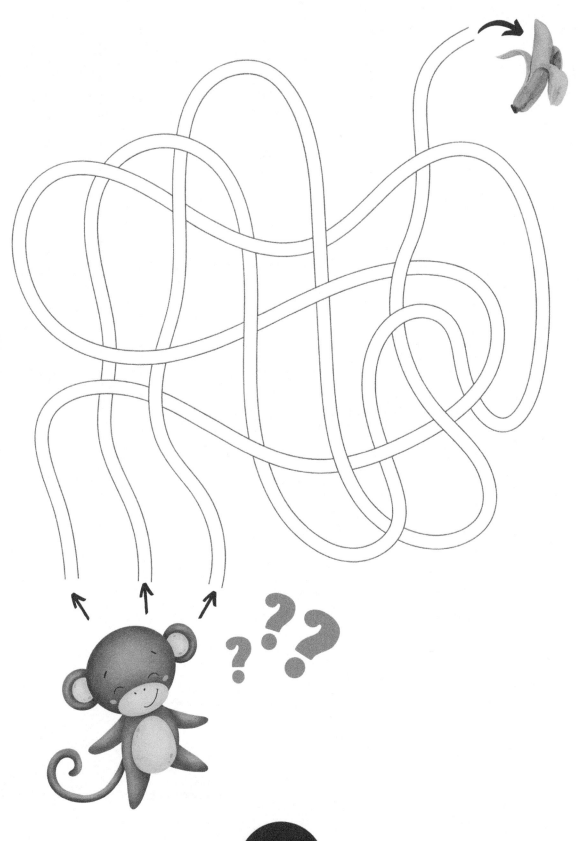

15

16

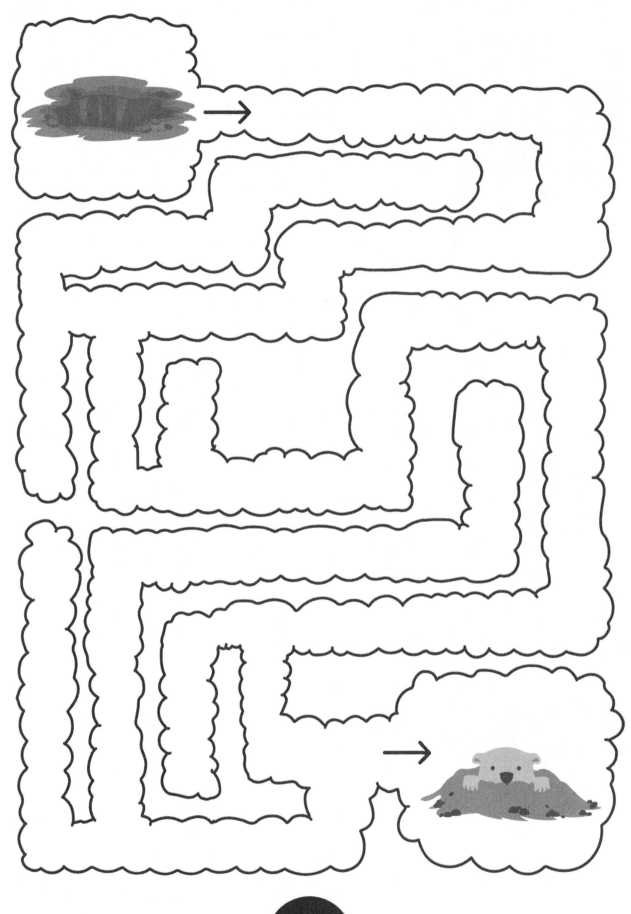

17

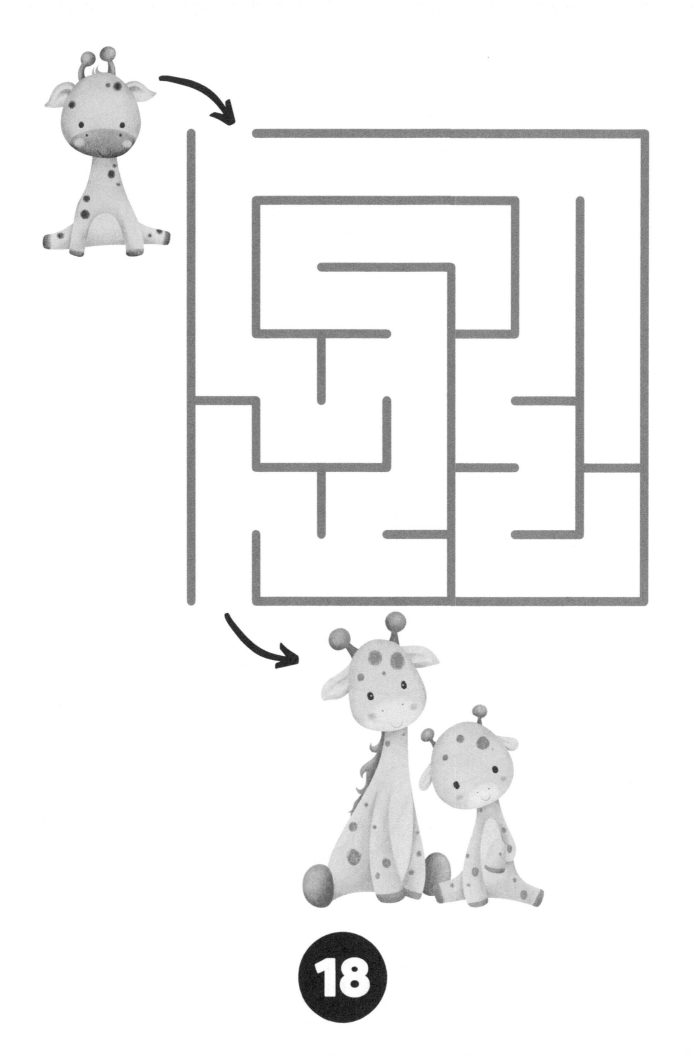

18

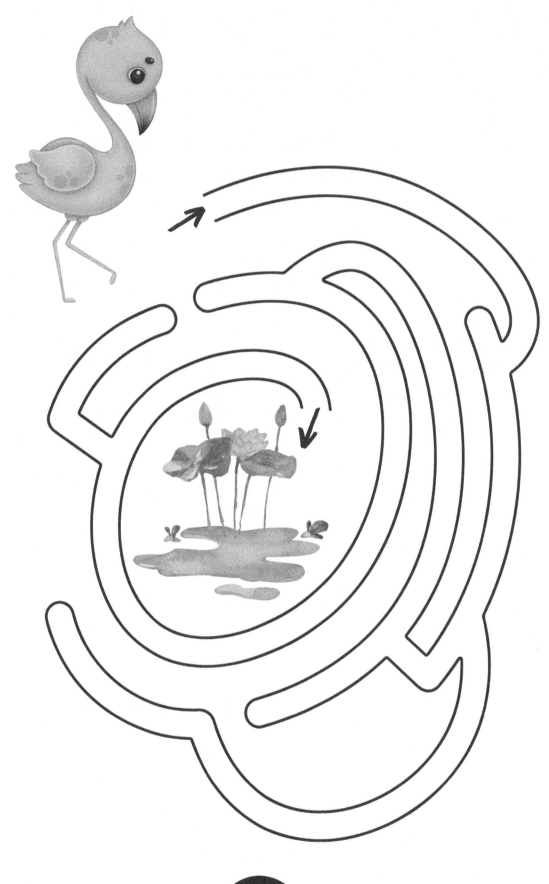

19

20

21

22

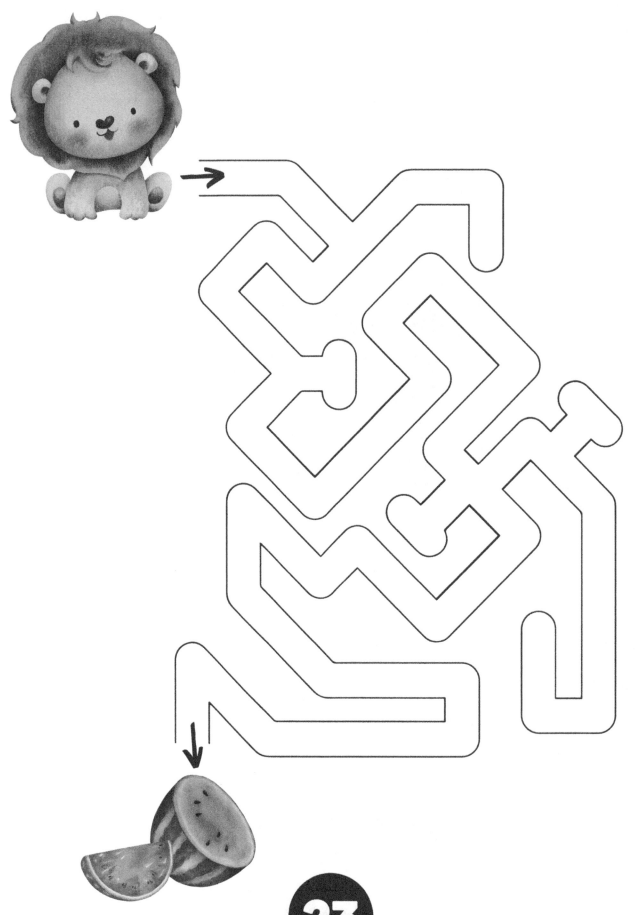

23

24

25

26

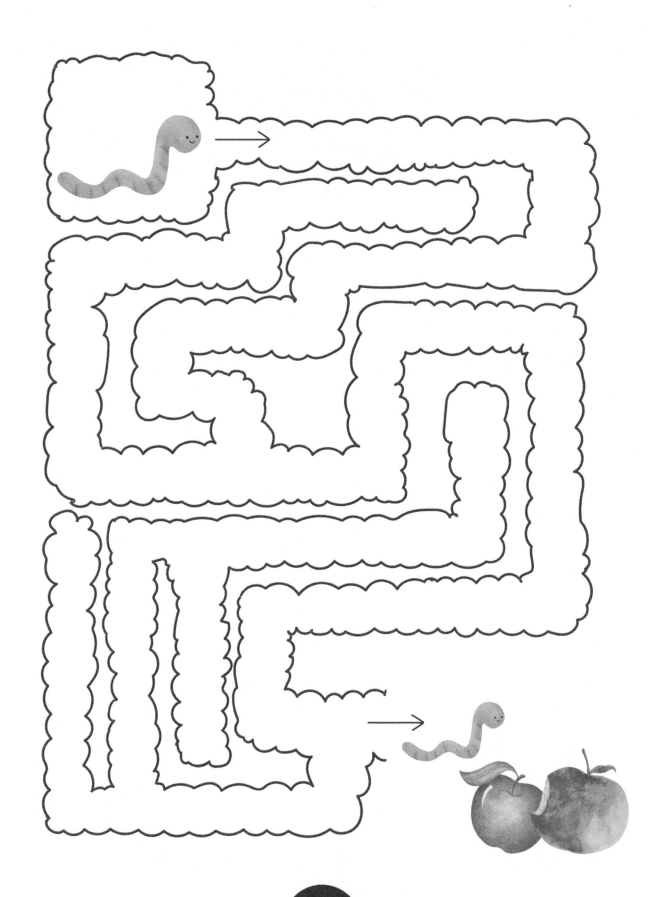

28

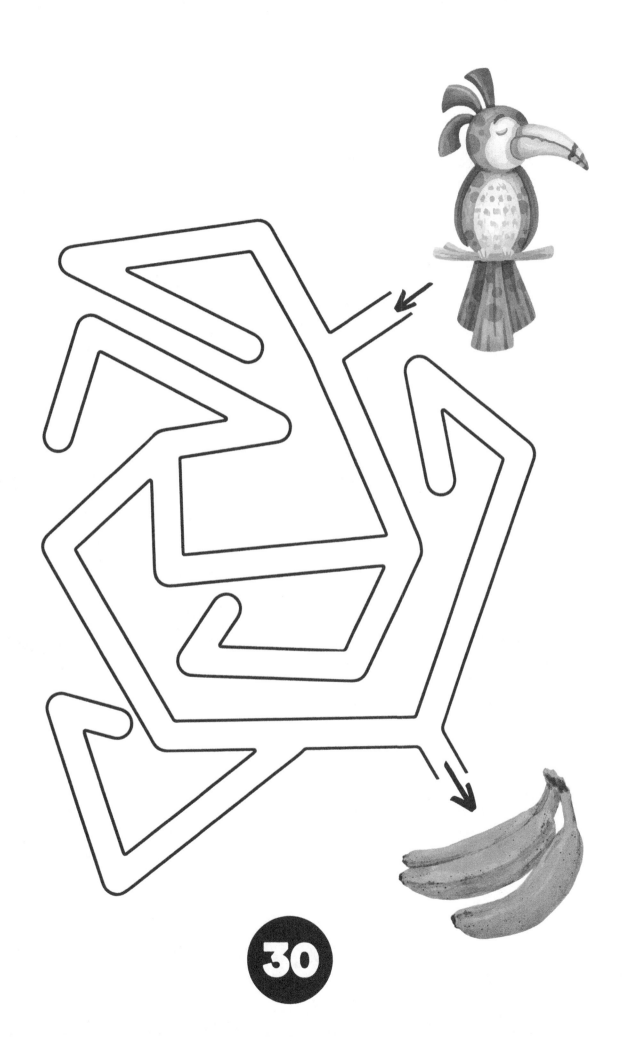

30

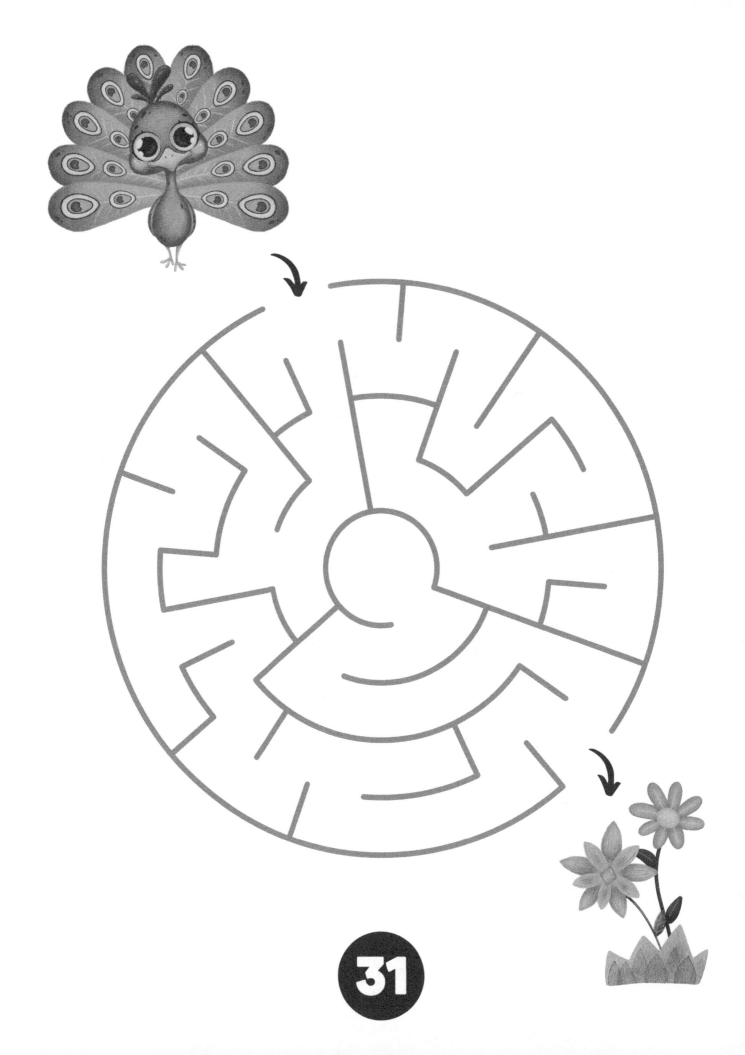

31

33

34

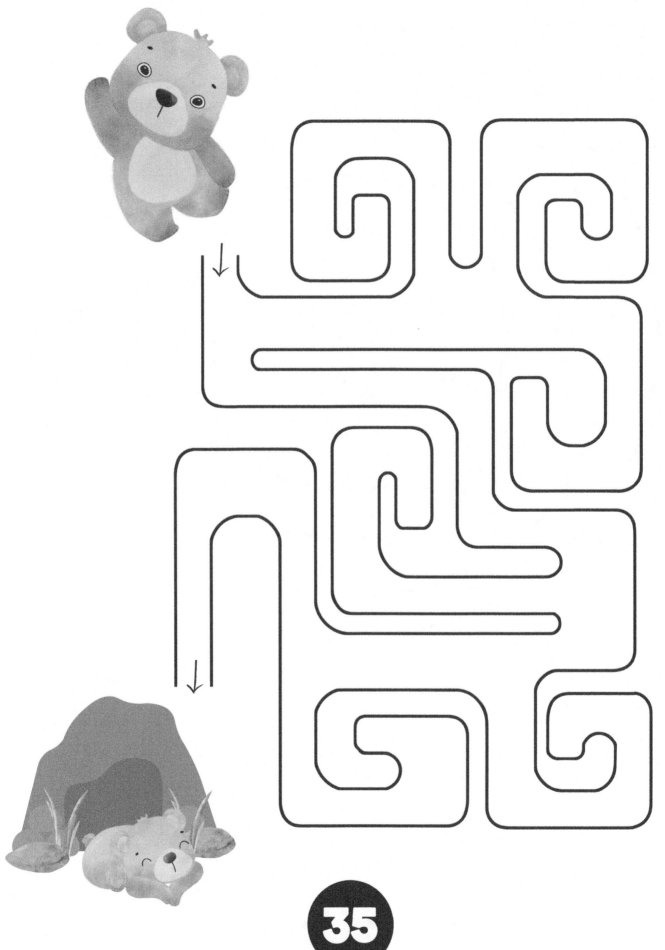

35

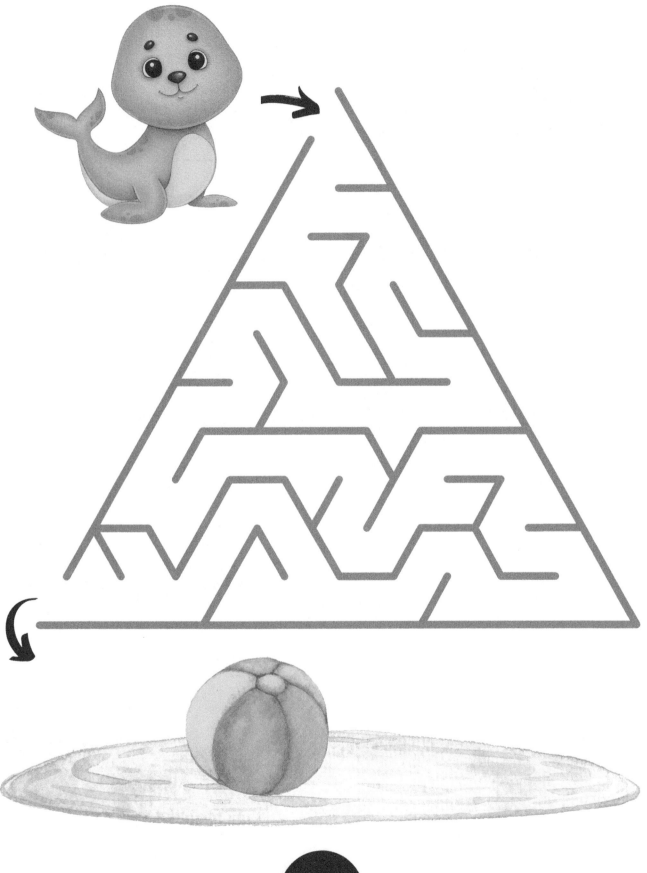

36

37

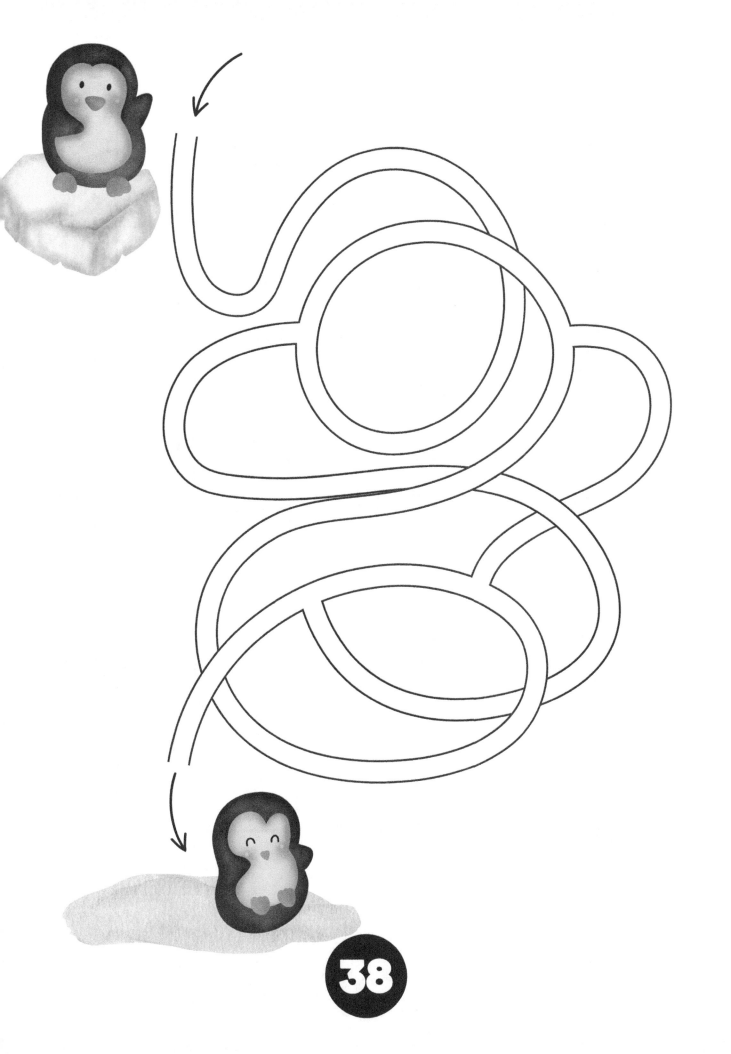

38

39

40

41

42

43

44

45

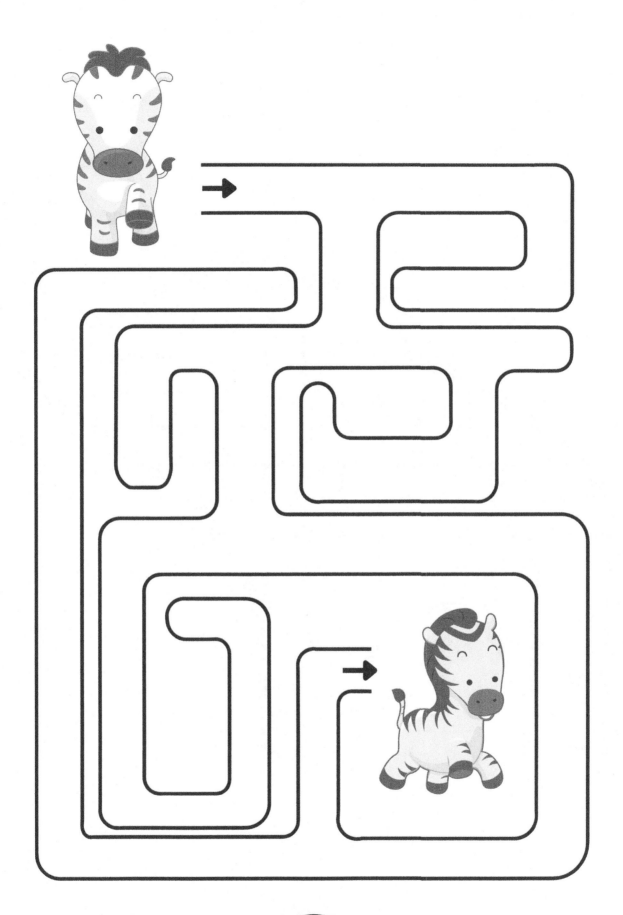

46

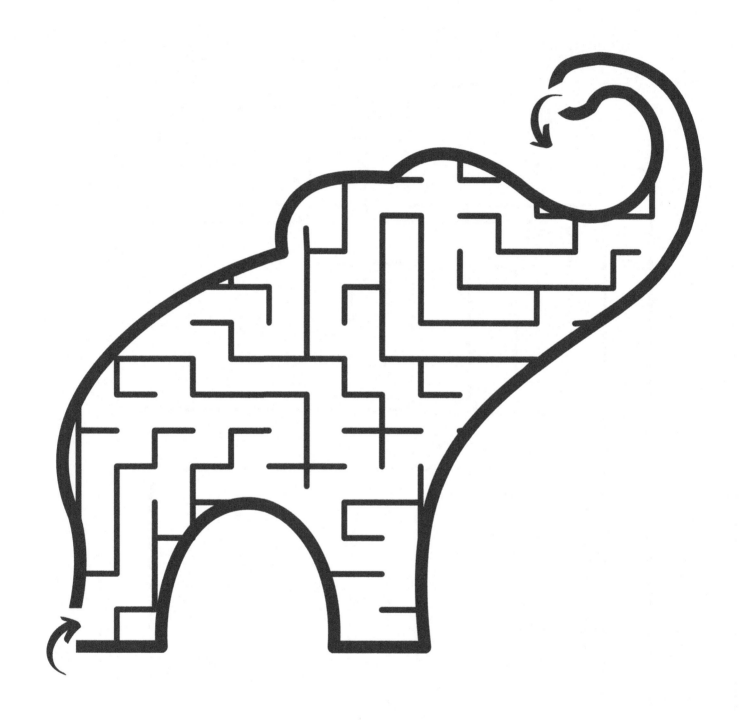

47

48

49

50

51

52

53

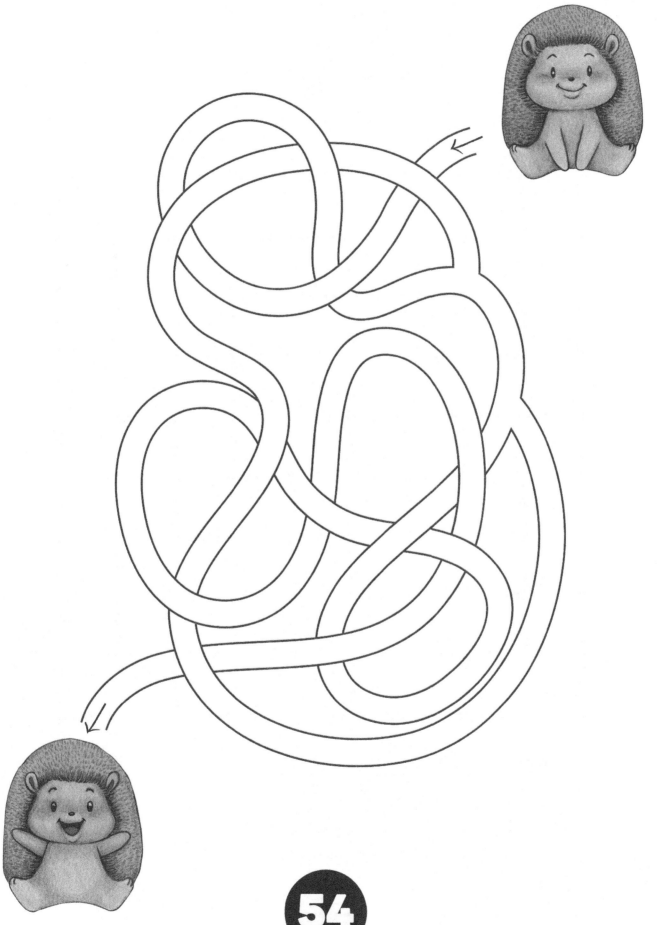

54

55

56

58

60

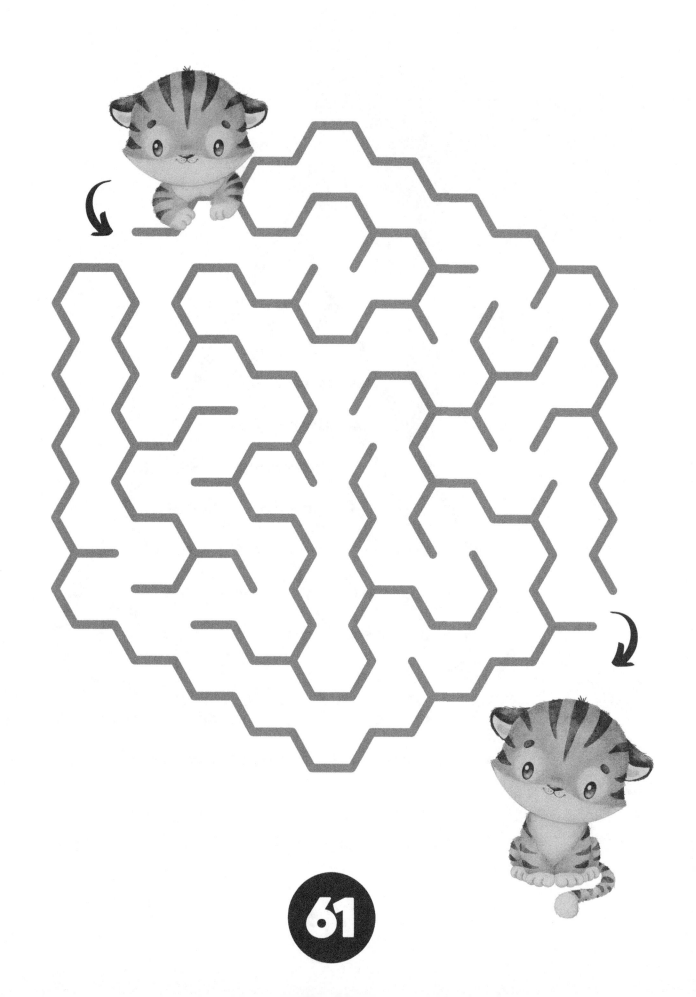

61

62

63

64

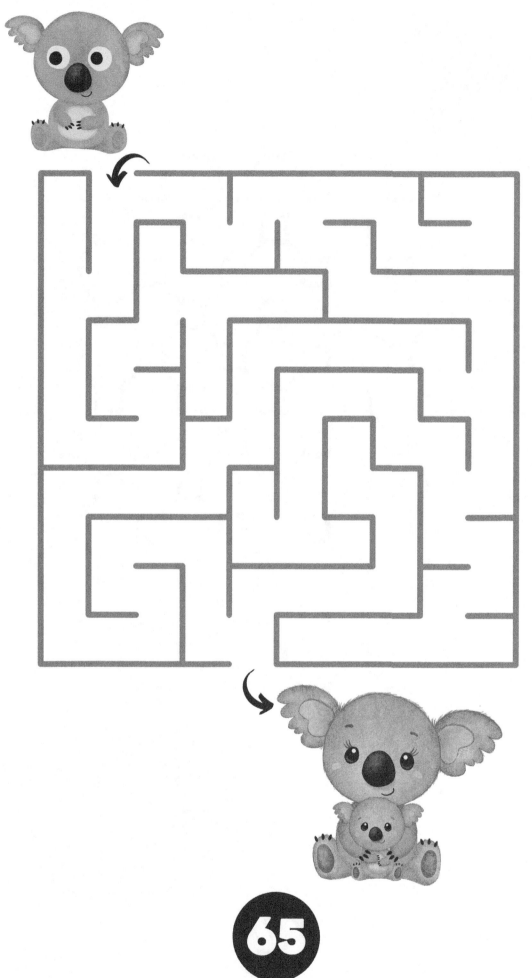

65

66

67

68

69

70

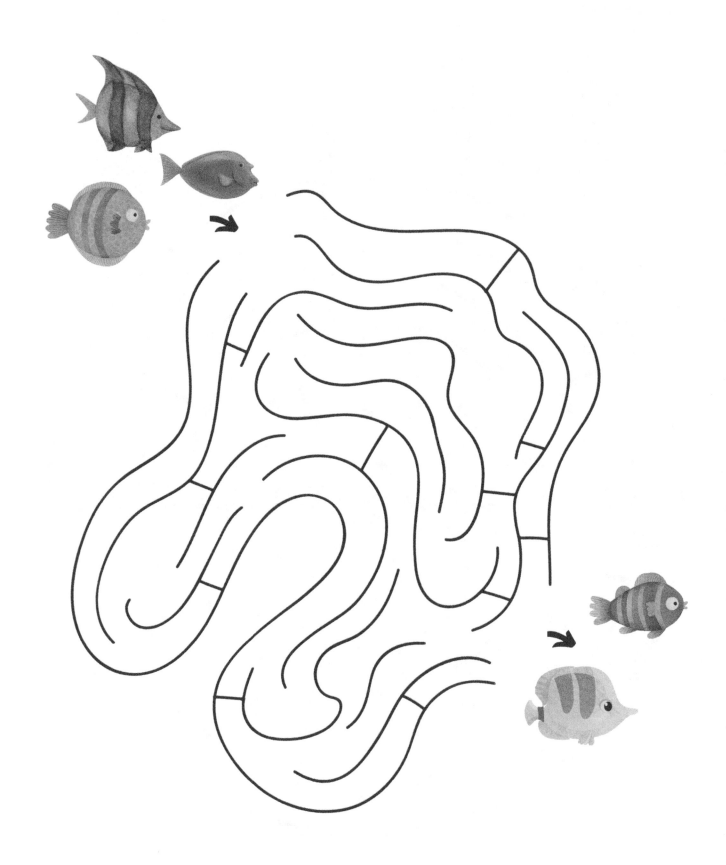

71

72

73

74

77

78

Great Job!

80

Solutions

1

2

3

4

Solutions

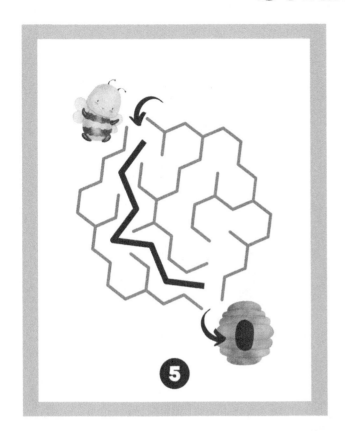

5

6

7

8

Solutions

9

10

11

12

Solutions

13

14

15

16

Solutions

17

18

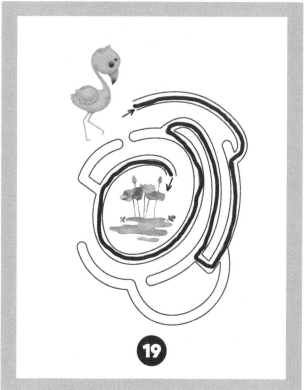

19

20

Solutions

21

22

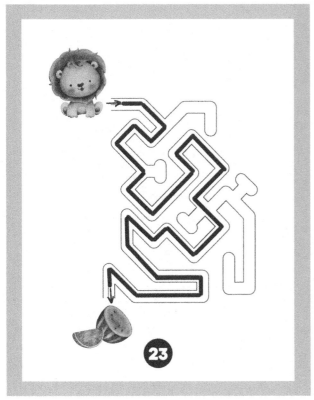

23

24

Solutions

25

26

27

28

Solutions

29

30

31

32

Solutions

33

34

35

36

Solutions

37

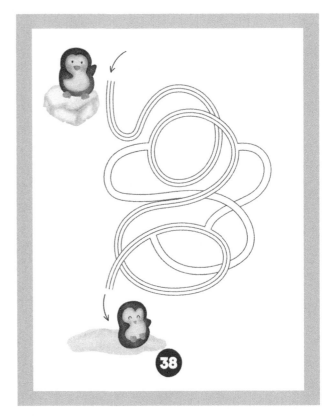

38

39

40

Solutions

41

42

43

44

Solutions

45

46

47

48

Solutions

49

50

51

52

Solutions

53

54

55

56

Solutions

57

58

59

60

Solutions

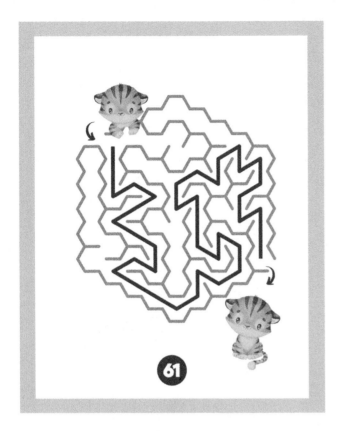

61

62

63

64

Solutions

65

66

67

68

Solutions

69

70

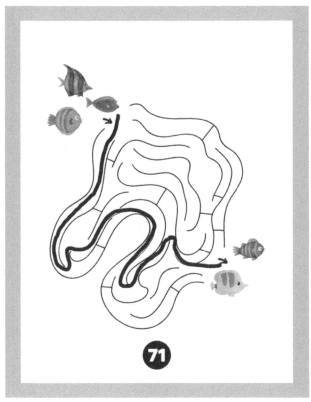

71

72

Solutions

73

74

75

76

Solutions

77

78

79

80

100

Zady Barnett

ACTIVITY BOOKS

Check out all our books at www.zadybarnett.com

Made in United States
North Haven, CT
03 June 2023

37332023R00057